Mr. & Mrs. R. G. Thompson
4545 Meadow Road
White Oaks
Edina, Minnesota 55424

4.95

# Here in Kennebunkport

1981

# *Here in Kennebunkport*

**Photographs by Lois Lowry**
**Text by Frederick H. Lewis**

**DURRELL PUBLICATIONS**

*Distributed by* The Stephen Greene Press
P.O. Box 1000, Brattleboro, Vermont 05301

Copyright © 1978 by Lois Lowry and Frederick H. Lewis

All rights reserved, including the right to
reproduce this book or portion thereof in any form.

FIRST EDITION

Production and Design by Bernard Schleifer

SBN: 911764–20–8

Printed in the United States of America

Kennebunkport, Maine

*T*WO CENTURIES AGO *and for many decades, Kennebunkport, Maine—originally named Cape Porpus, changed to Arundel, acquiring its present name in 1821—was a sea-faring community depending for its livelihood on the products of the ocean and upon a thriving shipbuilding industry. Schooners constructed along the banks of the Kennebunk River plied the trade routes of the seven seas.*

*Of the shipbuilding industry only small traces remain today; but the ocean's yield—lobsters, shrimp, fish—continues important to the town's economy. There is still sea-faring, for pleasure, by resident and visiting sloops, cruisers, and yachts that berth at marinas along the river or anchor in the snug harbor of Cape Porpoise.*

*Kennebunkport is a lively community of 2,500 people the year round, increasing ten-fold during the summer by temporary residents who own or rent, guests at the inns and hotels, and tourists. Of late, increasing numbers of city folk have been settling in the village for their retirement years.*

*We begin our photographic tour at Dock Square, the heart of Kennebunkport, and then roam around the 20 square miles of the town's present area.*

*P*RESIDING *over Dock Square, the center of village activity, is the Soldiers and Sailors Monument, erected in 1909 largely through the efforts of artist and architect Abbott Graves, a Kennebunkport resident.*

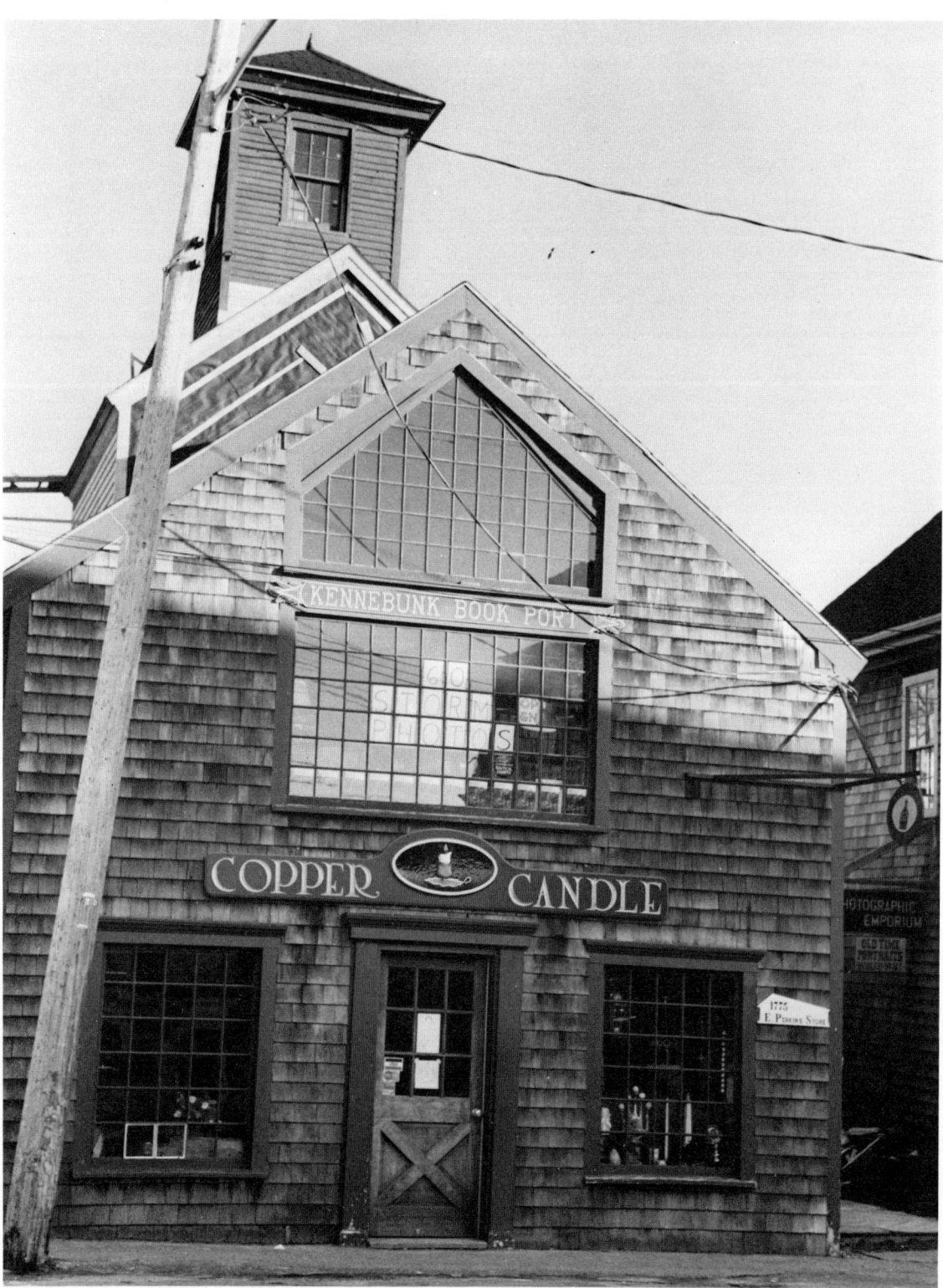

*BEFORE LEAVING Dock Square, note the 200 year old building now occupied by the Kennebunk Book Port and The Copper Candle. The story of this structure, and indeed of the residential area we are about to see, is described in "Rambles in the Port", an illuminating guide for three walking tours around the village.*

*O*N MAY 6, 1976, the National Park Service, through the Maine Historic Preservation Commission, designated the central residential area of Kennebunkport as an Historic Preservation District.

*Maine Street*

*P*ERHAPS THE MOST *distinctive feature of Kennebunkport is its array of stately vintage homes that date back as early as 1724, carefully and lovingly preserved by their successive owners.*

*Captain Lord Mansion*

*Pearl Street (Winter)*

*Pearl Street (Summer)*

*Pearl Street*

*Pearl Street*

ON YOUR HOUSE TOUR, *study the doorways. More than any other single feature they give a clue to the architectural period of construction. Authorities generally agree on four general periods: Colonial (1700-1795), Federal (1795–1830), Greek Revival (1830–1850), and Victorian (1850–1900). But there were other preceding and intermediate architectural influences: Cape, Georgian, Gothic, Renaissance, Italianate, Romanesque, Queen Anne, French Chateau, Neo-Colonial, Tudor, and Art Nouveau, that may be noted. For those wishing to pursue the subject, we suggest "200 Years of Maine Housing" from the Maine Historic Preservation Commission, Augusta, or "Maine Forms of American Architecture" from Downeast Publishers, Camden, Maine.*

*Maine Street*

Maine Street

*Elm Street*

*Pearl Street*

*Maine Street*

Union Street

*North Street*

*Pearl Street*

*Maine Street*

*Pearl Street*

*Dock Square*

Dock Square, Ocean Avenue

*I*N COLONIAL TIMES, *the hub of community life was the meeting house. It served not only as a house of worship, but variously as town hall, library, recreation center, general court, and sometimes even jail.*

The Christopher Wren design steeple of the South Congregational Church

*Saint Ann's Episcopal Church*

*H*ISTORY BUFFS *can have a field day by travelling out North Street a mile or so from Dock Square to the Kennebunkport Historical Society. Open every day during the summer, on display are pictures, documents, maps, costumes, furniture and other evidences of the town's past. Housed in a separate building is The Clark Shipbuilding Collection.*

*E*VEN THOUGH *the great schooner shipbuilding days are over, boats of all sorts remain a central feature of the life of Kennebunkport. Craftsmen are still at work constructing smaller vessels. The sturdy craft of the lobstermen anchor in the river and at Cape Porpoise, with their entourage of gulls. And the sleek proud boats of the pleasure sailors cast their shadows and reflections onto the water.*

*Government wharf*

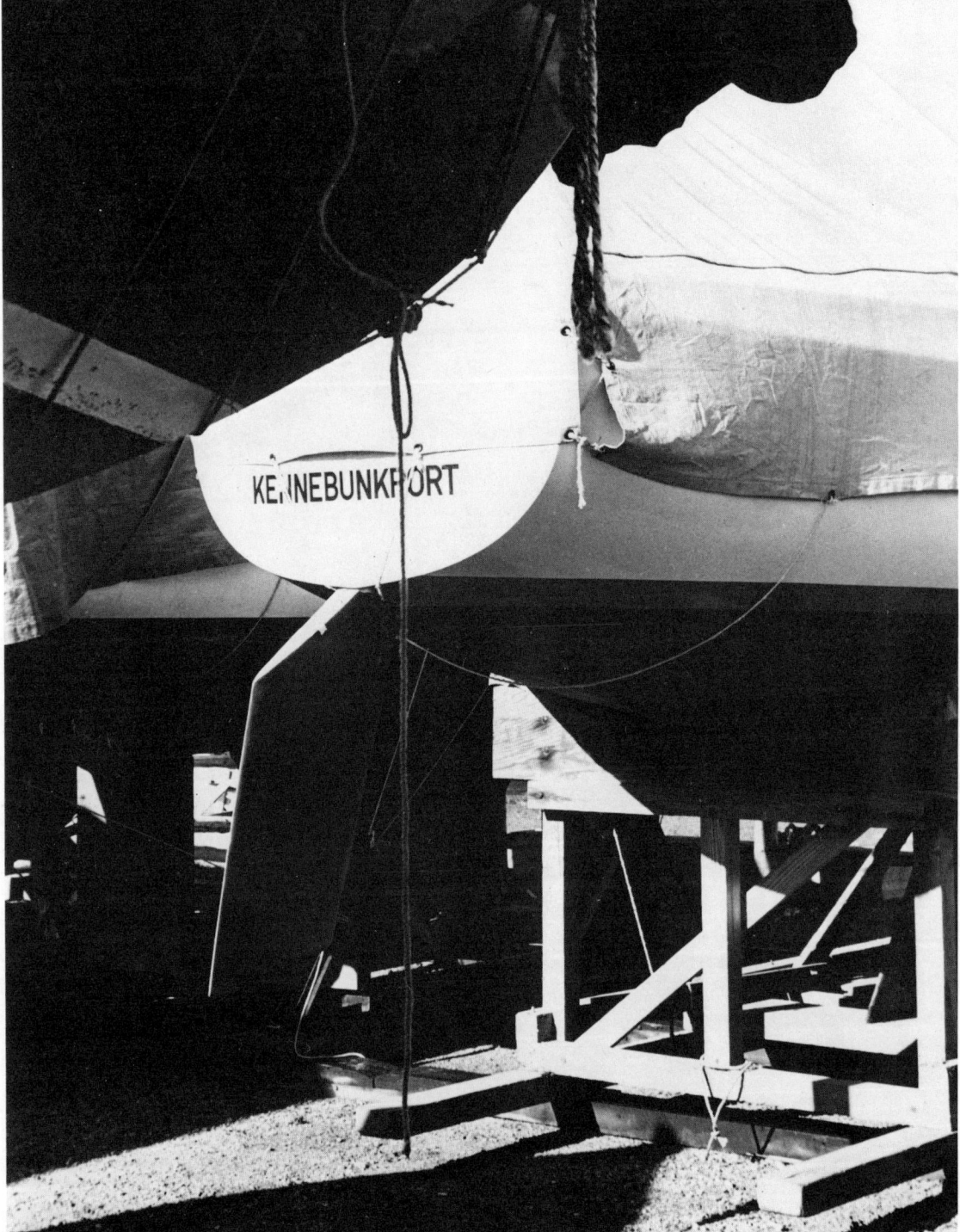

*Parsons Way, Ocean Avenue*

*K*ENNEBUNKPORT *was "discovered" as a summer resort in the early 1890s by a group of well-to-do Boston, New York, and Philadelphia families who built many of the grand mansions extending for three miles along Ocean Avenue. But not even the most impressive homes can match the awesome grandeur of the sea against the coastline here.*

*Spouting Rock*

Vice President George Bush's Summer Home

*A*LONG WITH *numerous smaller inns, three notable hotels welcome the summer visitor to* Kennebunkport.

*The Colony, Ocean Avenue*

*The Nonantum, Ocean Avenue*

*The Shawmut Inn, Turbot's Creek*

*The River Club, Boat House*

*The River Club, Casino*

*K*ENNEBUNKPORT *has long been a magnet for artists and writers. The works of its residents—writers such as Booth Tarkington, Kenneth Roberts, Lin Yutang, and Margaret Deland; such artists as Peggy Bacon, Abbott Graves, Roger Deering, and Eliot O'Hara—can be found in libraries and galleries all over the world. The many artists who are permanent residents are augmented by others who flock here in the summer.*

BOOTH TARKINGTON did much of his writing aboard his two-masted schooner "Regina," for many years moored here by his boathouse.

"Rocky Pastures", the home of the late Kenneth Roberts, was ravaged by fire in 1975. Extensive renovation by its new owners has restored its beauty.

The Louis T. Graves Memorial Library on Maine Street houses a fine collection of paintings by the late Abbott Graves.

*Kennebunkport resident, resting*

*Kennebunkport resident, resting*

*S*EVERAL MILES BY SEA *from Dock Square, but only a couple by Route 9, lies the quiet settlement around the protected harbor of Cape Porpoise, the home of lobstermen whose boats chug past the Goat Island lighthouse at daybreak and return with their catch each afternoon. Cape Porpoise is in the township of Kennebunkport.*

*Cape Porpoise*

*Cape Porpoise*

*Cape Porpoise*

*Four miles east of Cape Porpoise and still in the township of Kennebunkport, on Route 9 is the much photographed landmark, the Clock Farm. Here one turns right to Goose Rocks Beach, regarded by many as the loveliest beach on the Maine coast.*

*The Clock Farm*

*Goose Rocks Beach*

THE BEACH IN SUMMER: *a place for solitary strolls, sand-castle friendships, and the toe-tingling excitement of gentle surf.*

*T*HE WIDELY SCATTERED *settlements of Kennebunkport are protected by four modern fire companies manned by well-trained volunteers.*

*For old times sake, Chief Royal Smith exercises the Goose Rocks Beach vintage fire engine acquired in 1927.*

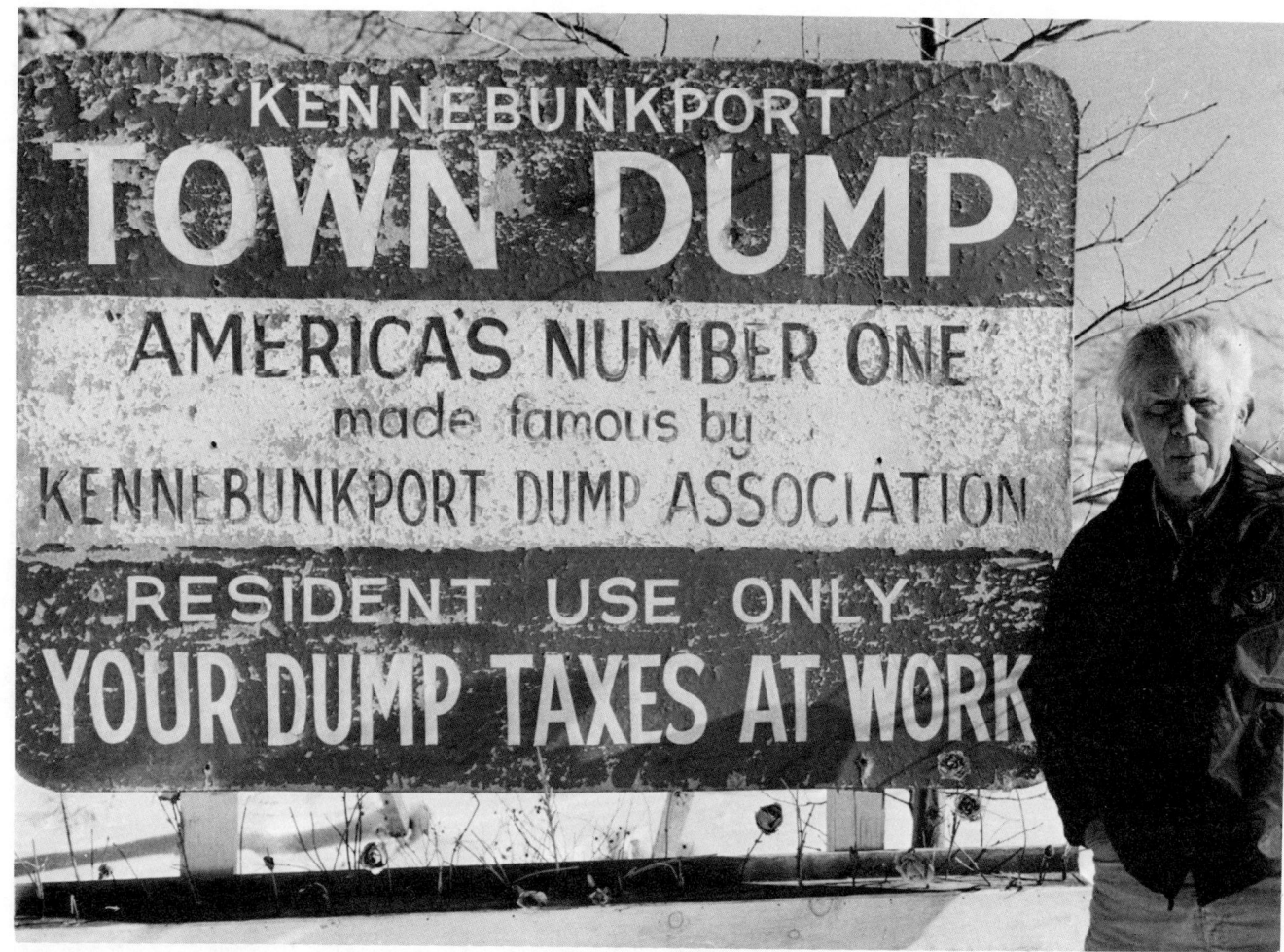

*Edward Mayo*

*T*RAVELLING BACK *from Goose Rocks Beach to Dock Square by an alternate route, one comes upon the entrance to the Kennebunkport Town Dump, proclaimed by the Association whose name it bears as America's Number One Dump. Founder and president of the KDA, humorist, raconteur, and artist is Edward Mayo, whose antics have won him a nationwide following.*\*

\*Mr. Mayo is the author of the amusing "Dump Watchers' Handbook" available at the Kennebunk Book Port.

*B*ACK AT DOCK SQUARE, *where restored nineteenth-century buildings now house craft shops, restaurants, and boutiques . . . where walking, browsing, and people-watching are a treat in summer, and where, when Fall comes, quiet simplicity returns, here in Kennebunkport.*

*B*EAUTIFULLY CRAFTED *signs that are visible throughout Kennebunkport reflect the meticulous care with which residents have sought to weld the past to the present. This is not a neon and tinsel town, but one of quiet charm, sunwashed summer color, and the crisp, clean brilliance of snow.*

*M*ISSED ANYTHING? *Take another tour. And enjoy yourself,* here in Kennebunkport.